Trouble at Home

Written & Illustrated by

Stephanie A. Kilgore-White

DP KIDS PRESS

244 5th Ave, Suite G200
New York, NY 10001
Phone: 646-233-4366
www.DocUmeantPublishing.com

Published by
DP Kids Press
a division of DocUmeant Publishing
244 5th Avenue, Suite G-200
NY, NY 10001

646-233-4366

All Scripture quotations are taken from the Holman Christian Standard Bible, copyright 1999, 2000, 2002, 2003, by Holman Bible Publishers. Used by permission.

Digitally colored by Ginger Marks, DocUmeantDesigns.com

Library of Congress: 2021931204

ISBN: 978-1-950075-38-6 (pbk)
ISBN: 978-1-950075-39-3 (ePub)

As I think about my personal childhood, I realize there was trouble in my home. As a young girl I couldn't understand it and no adult took time to explain what was happening to me. It was very troubling and had a haunting effect on me for years. Later, I understood that things were quite disturbing. However, my mom did her best to help us survive. So mom, this book is dedicated to you. Thank you for keeping us out of harm's way and for raising us up in a home where we felt safe and secure. You sacrificed a lot, but you did it!

I also give thanks to God and my Savior, Jesus Christ who came on the scene in my life personally, at a young age, to help me get through life's struggles with grace and ease. He was my Charity and my Champ. He loved me through it all. So God, you get the glory for bringing me through!

To every young person who is reading this book and has suffered a life of abuse and neglect, or who has experienced trouble at home, this book is for you. Just know that you are not alone. God desires that you have an abundant life that is free from all the heartache that is experienced when there is trouble in the home. Draw upon Him. Also, seek help from a trusted friend and never experience it alone.

May God use this story to bring discovery, help, sensitivity, healing and care to all who have or are experiencing trouble in your home.

I Peter 5:7
"Cast your care upon Him, because he cares for you."

Love and blessings!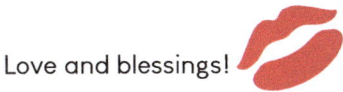

This story is about a beautiful and loving family of four, Who many people who knew them had come to adore.

They had a nice house, fancy car,
and other material things,
Which was what others believed
true happiness brings.

However, behind closed doors there were problems within,

The dad's drinking and abuse was his ultimate sin.

The dad drank before, during and after work each day,

While the mom lived in fear and would constantly pray.

The children witnessed their dad drunk every day of their lives,

Which caused their home to be filled with pain and strife.

One day after
school the dad
violently abused
his wife,
And afterwards
he threatened
to take his own
life.

The children were fearful,
so they called the police,

Since they knew
this violence had to
abruptly cease.

The mom was rushed to the hospital, the dad went straight to jail,

He would be there a long time, without any hope to make bail.

While both parents were away the children were placed in another home, Until their mom fully recovered because they couldn't be left alone.

The children were sad and cried themselves to sleep each night,

As they prayed to God to make everything alright.

The next day God sent
Charity and her brother
Champ from above,

With a mission to show the children his comfort and love.

Charity and Champ spent time with the children each day, Demonstrating God's love through their time at play.

Their mom eventually got better and the children returned to her care,
They no longer had to fear since their dad was no longer there.

Within months Charity and Champ's
mission had finally come to an end,
The family was seemingly doing fine,
but their hearts needed time to mend.

Charity and Champ watched over the
family, helping them to all heal,
From the abuse they had suffered
which was a terrible ordeal.

Charity and Champ want you to
know that if abuse is in your home,
Seek help from a trusted friend,
but never experience it alone.

Just know that God is with you,
He will always come to your aid
Trust in Him to lovingly
protect you and never be afraid,

Because God's desire is to keep you safe
and protected from all harm
So if there's trouble in your home, please
sound the boisterous alarm,

Words from the Author

I hope that you've enjoyed this book, but oh there's so much more. There will be others soon to come, featuring the character that you'll come to adore.

Charity wants to be your friend, you can introduce her to others too!

Join with me at my website, where you'll find out what's in store.

https://heavensdivinekiss.com/

If you have enjoyed this book, please let me hear from you. Also, be sure to leave a positive review on your favorite bookstore's website.

anne.white
.399488

stephan69239406

heavensdivine
kiss1377

hdkiss1377